CONTENTS

I0625089

The Mystery of the $50,000 Trout Festival Prize

by: Joe & Celina Castañeda

Find the latest Ktown Mystery book at:
www.ktownmysteries.com

Interior Artwork by: Bill Versnick

Cover design by: Keith Parker

ISBN-13:978-1-943635-18-4

We dedicate this book to all the parents and children who enjoy a good bedtime story.

ACKNOWLEDGMENTS

Sadly, books never write themselves, and this first book of the K-Town Mystery Series is no exception. Instead, as usual, it was an amazing group of people that came together to make this project a reality, and not enough of them will be mentioned here! However, we do want to single out a few. Much gratitude goes out to Sharilyn Lewis for editing most of this manuscript. A big thanks is also due to our Secret Reader in Tacoma, WA who read the story early on and provided some great insight. Bill Versnick is the man behind the interior artwork, and Keith Parker was a master, yet again, at cover design. And of course, the Wife/Mom of this project listened to, and read, this manuscript dozens of times and offered encouragement and insight: thank you Traci!

1 BREAK IN

Jordan Joy found it hard to sit still as she looked out of her 5th grade classroom window, hoping the sun might break through the clouds on this late April day. It's Thursday, and Friday is one of the more exciting days in her small town in northern Michigan (or "NoMi" as she liked to call it): the start of the National Trout Festival. For over 80 years Kalkaska, Michigan, has been home to this celebration of the start of trout season, and every year there is an air of excitement and energy as Trout Festival approaches.

Of course, in Northern Michigan the weather can be as crazy and unpredictable as Jordan's 5th grade PE class, so she has celebrated Trout Fest in everything from snow, to rain, to nearly 80-degree spring weather! Although, It really doesn't matter what the weather is like, since everyone celebrates Trout Fest in her town because...well...because it's what they do.

Part of the fun of the tradition is that the school week is cut short; Friday is a half day so the full celebration can begin a little early. As Jordan Joy (known as "JJ" to many of her friends) looked out the window at the bare trees and cloudy sky, she was excited thining about the short day awaiting her tomorrow, the carnival rides and special events that would take place over the weekend, and of course, the grand parade with over 100 different floats. She loves Trout Fest.

Jordan snapped back to reality when she heard her teacher, Ms. Hermom, ask, "Jordan, what are you most looking forward to with Trout Festival this weekend?"

"I can't wait for the parade. I love the parade. And I love the special events like the poetry contest and the animal shows. I also love the carnival rides. And I love the smell of the elephant ears, and I love..."

"Thank you, Jordan," said Ms. Hermom with a laugh. "It seems you like just about everything related to this weekend!"

Jordan blushed a little as the whole class laughed at her enthusiasm. They were right, though; she did love everything about Trout Festival.

When school ended, Jordan walked out the large front door of Cherry Street Intermediate School and waited for her mom to pick her up. The big brick building sat right on the street next to houses where several of Jordan's classmates lived, and just down the street from the county hospital. Right on time, Mrs C, who often subbed in the other Kalkaska schools, rolled up in the familiar dark green minivan.

Jordan said goodbye to her friends and ran down the seven concrete steps leading away from the school.

As soon as she hopped in the van she began talking about Trout Fest. The two of them stopped at the high school, a new, more modern looking building, and then the middle school, with its big gymnasium visible from the parking lot, so they could pick up her brother, Joe, and her sister, Erin. Then everyone returned home to enjoy a quick snack before tackling some homework. It was hard for Jordan to focus while she was so excited for Friday.

As Jordan finished her schoolwork, her dad returned home from the office and came up the stairs into their apartment. Jordan's mom greeted her dad with kiss (Jordan and her sister always teased them, "Gross! No kissing in front of the kids!") and then he shared some news.

"On my way home today I was listening to the radio, and learned something interesting about one of the first county festivals here in Kalkaska."

At the word "festival," Jordan jumped to her feet and ran to hear her dad's story.

"In 1909, almost 30 years before the first Trout Festival, when your mother was just a young girl ..." Jordan's mom smirked and then snapped a towel at her dad. He jumped back, laughing, but continued his story.

"...The county fair held some contests and events where very significant prizes were given. For several years they had a writing contest, and the winners received special books or journals as prizes. Local teachers and newspaper editors judged each entry. In one particular year, the prize was a special, autographed, leather-bound copy of Longfellow's *Evangeline*, and the winner of each category received a copy."

"Apparently the copies of those books are very valuable today, maybe worth as much as $50,000!"

"Wow!" Jordan exclaimed. She loved books, and had read hundreds of them already, but she was fairly certain she had never read a book worth $50,000.

"Most people believe there are only one or two copies of those books around today," continued her day, "which is part of the reason they are so valuable. Up until last night, one of them was here in Kalkaska."

"What do you mean, 'up until last night'?" asked Jordan's brother, Joe.

"Well, the Blanco family owned one of those books." Jordan knew the Blanco family well, as one of her best friends at school was Abby Blanco. "Last night their house was broken into, and the book was stolen," explained Mr. C.

Jordan gasped as her father continued. "Mr. Blanco didn't know how much the book was worth until he realized it was the only thing taken from their house. When he reported the oddity of the crime to the police, telling them, 'All they took was an old book,' the police investigated the title and discovered that the old book was worth over $50,000."

"The timing of this theft is especially surprising, because Sunday Mr. Blanco was going to display the book at the conclusion of Trout Fest as part of the county tribute to more than 100 years of festivals in Kalkaska. It was supposed to be part of a grand finale before the fireworks show that ends the celebration."

Jordan was shocked that her friend's home was the target of a crime, but if there was one thing she loved more than Trout Fest, it was solving a good mystery. And by the sounds of it, a good mystery just showed up in Kalkaska!

2 PIZZA, HORSES,
AND A FIRST CLUE

Jordan put away her schoolbooks, then asked her mom how long she had until dinner was ready. Her mom reminded her that Thursday night was pizza night, and tonight they would be making homemade pizzas with their friends, the Simons, at 6pm. The Simons had two children, a boy and girl, but both of them were much older and already in college. That didn't bother Jordan though, she loved going over to their house for visits, as the Simons had been good family friends since Jordan and her family had moved to Michigan a few years back. Seeing that she had about an hour until they left for their house, Jordan went to work on solving this crime.

Her first order of business was to learn about the contest from the first county fair that came 30 years before Trout Festival. She pulled up a massive book her family stored on the bottom shelf, one that helped them understand the culture of Kalkaska, Michigan, when they first moved in. The book was called *Big Trout Black Gold,* and it was full of information about Northern Michigan and the history of Kalkaska.

In the book she found details about the writing contest held the first year of the fair. Back in 1909 it was simply called the Kalkaska County Fair, and she learned that winners from different categories included the Morris family, the Wisdom family and, of course, the Blanco family. In fact, it appeared that the Wisdom and Blanco families each won a number of the prizes the first year of the event.

She chuckled when she read about the "Baby Contest" that included judging of the cutest one-year-old baby in the county. Based on her family pictures, Jordan was sure her sister Erin would have won that contest when she was a baby. Erin was blond-haired, blue-eyed and adorable as a baby (and just as pretty today, too), while Jordan and Joe had both been plump. Her dad always said they were "Michelin" babies … whatever that meant.

Jordan pulled out a dark pink notebook with a colorful butterfly on the cover. This was her detective notebook, and she wrote down facts and family names from the *Big Trout Black Gold* book. She was always careful to write down anything that might prove helpful in solving a case.

Next, Jordan called her best friend, Emmie, a girl she loved to drag along into her crime solving adventures. Emmie had also just finished her homework and was always happy to hear from Jordan.

"Slow down, JJ—what on earth are you so excited about?" asked Emmie. Jordan was always a fast talker, but when she was excited, her words came out even faster.

"You know how I am when I learn of another mystery —I just can't contain it. And this one seems very interesting to me! Think about it. This book, from one of the first county-wide festivals in Kalkaska, was stolen less than 48 hours before the start of another festival. That cannot be a coincidence," said Jordan.

"I've learned that nothing is a coincidence with you," teased Emmie, "and besides, what could make Trout Festival any more fun than to have a mystery to solve, too?"

"Exactly!" replied Jordan. "I have about an hour until we have to leave for the Simons' for pizza night. Can you come over and help me gather some data about this book?"

"Only if I can have some of your mom's amazing brownies while we work!" exlaimed Emmie. Both girls laughed, and in just a few minutes Emmie knocked on Jordan's door. She lived in the same apartment complex as Jordan, and sometimes it was hard to know where each girl lived because they spent so much time in each other's homes.

"Hi, Emmie!" Jordan said as she bounded down the stairs, threw the door open, nearly jumped into her friend's arms and began hugging Emmie. JJ was one of the shortest girls in her grade, and Emmie was just slightly taller, which was why people sometimes thought they were twin sisters. Emmie was fond of wearing brightly colored clothes, and the lime green t-shirt and tie-dyed skirt she was wearing, fit her bubbly personality perfectly.

"Well, hi, JJ, I miss you too. It has been nearly an hour since I saw you at school," Emmie teased as she hugged her friend. "Now, let's get down to business," she said, as the girls tossed their shoes into the front closet and headed upstairs to Jordan's room. "Where are the brownies?" she asked with a smile.

Not to disappoint, Jordan's mom had a plate with two brownies she had warmed in the microwave, along with two glasses of milk.

"Hi, Mrs. C.," said Emmie as she sat down at the table. "Thanks for the brownies, but where is JJ's plate?"

"Not so fast!" squealed Jordan as she slid next to Emmie on the bench-style seat at the kitchen table. The girls devoured their brownies and milk in a few moments. The brownies practically melted in their hands; the gooey chocolaty center was the perfect temperature. Then they hopped up to go into Jordan's room.

"Just a moment, ladies ..." they heard Jordan's mom say in that special tone that only a mother can use. Without missing a beat both girls stopped on the wood floor, sliding in their matching purple striped socks for a few feet, and made u-turns back into the kitchen. They giggled as they grabbed the brownie plate and empty milk glasses, rinsed them and set them in the dishwasher, knowing immediately why Mrs. C. had called them back to the table.

"Thank you," said Mrs. C. with a smile, as the two bouncy girls whirled back around on course for Jordan's room.

"OK," said Jordan in a way that showed she was ready to focus on the case. "Here's what I have so far. Back in the 1900s, before Trout Festival was even called Trout Fest, they had a contest for writers. You could write in several categories, and the winners received really cool prizes."

"Local reporters, authors, and newspaper editors were the judges, and at the end of the week a winner was chosen from each category. This particular year, 1909, the winners received an autographed, leather-bound copy of *Evangeline* as a prize."

"That would be a great prize," said Emmie.

"I know, right?" replied Jordan. "Well, you'll never guess what this has to do with the mystery I'm working on."

"You're right," giggled Emmie, "I won't guess." Emmie's green eyes sparkled with expectation.

"Last night, right here in Kalkaska, there was a break-in at the Blancos' house, and they were robbed."

"You mean Abby's family? Is everything OK?" asked Emmie.

"Yes," said Jordan reassuringly, "everything is fine. In fact, the break-in was so strange because the thief only took one item."

"Wait, let me guess: Abby's Littlest Pet Shop collection," Emmie said with fear that she'd be right.

"Thankfully, not that!" replied Jordan. "Actually, as hard as it is to imagine, there was something even more valuable in the Blancos' house: one of those prize books from the 1909 Kalkaska Country Fair writing contest!"

"Wow! Someone in Abby's family won that contest in 1909? That's awesome! We know someone famous, JJ!" shrieked Emmie.

"You are so goofy sometimes," laughed Jordan. "Abby's great, great grandmother was the one who won the contest, and the book has been in the family ever since."

"After Mr. Blanco reported the theft, the police looked into the crime, wondering why only one book was taken. They discovered that the missing book was worth a lot of money. Wanna guess how much?"

Emmie loved guessing games. "$2,000?"

"Higher," said Jordan.

"Higher? How about $5,000?" returned Emmie.

"Even higher," replied Jordan.

"What? I've never heard of a book being worth so much! Just tell me; now I'm dying to know," said Emmie with anticipation.

"The book," said Jordan, "is worth over $50,000! Mr. Blanco had planned to display it at the Kaliseum on Sunday night, right before the fireworks finale."

"Wow!" exclaimed Emmie.

"So we have a real mystery on our hands, Emmie. A 100-year-old, $50,000 Kalkaska County Fair prize goes missing two days before Trout Festival, where it is supposed to be on display. I'm certain the timing is not a coincidence and, if you ask me, we are going need to solve this crime before Trout Festival is over on Sunday."

"That's three days away," replied Emmie.

"I know," said Jordan, as she ran her fingers through her shoulder length hair, "that's why I called you over. We're going to have to work fast."

The girls spent the next thirty minutes poring over some old history books about Kalkaska, trying to figure out who might have some sort of connection to the old case. The most obvious place to start was with the names of the other contest winners or, as Jordan said, "those who might have finished second place, and didn't receive the prize."

"What?" asked Emmie with a little suspicion in her voice. "Are you suggesting that a family member of a second place finisher might have stolen the prize one hundred years later? That seems a little crazy."

"Crazy or not, it's at least a place to start," said Jordan matter-of-factly.

As the girls made some final notes, Jordan's mom entered the room to let Emmie know she needed to leave, because Jordan's family was heading over to the Simons' house for dinner.

"OK, thanks for letting me come over, Mrs. C., and thanks for the delicious brownie," said Emmie politely.

"Any time, sweetie," replied Mrs. C., "and be sure to tell your mom 'Hi' for me and that I look forward to seeing her at Bible study on Monday."

"I will," said Emmie. The two girls hugged goodbye and promised to exchange notes tomorrow at school. Emmie said she would call Abby and ask about coming over to see the crime scene with JJ after school, before the girls headed to the Trout Fest Midway to check out the carnival rides and dinner options at the food booths.

"Great idea, Emmie, and please ask her to not let anyone touch the book shelf, or anything nearby, until we get there," urged Jordan.

"I will let her know that Detective JJ is hot on the trail of the thief," she said with smile.

Emmie left and, shortly after, Jordan and her family departed for the Simons'. Even though Jordan loved being at their farmhouse around all the animals, she found herself caught up in thought about the case. She had so many questions, and Jordan was afraid that if her theory was right about the timing of this crime, she wouldn't have enough time to solve this mystery.

As they finished their delicious homemade pizzas and started on dessert, Mr. Simon called to Jordan, "Hey, Peanut (his special name for her), are you excited for the start of Trout Festival?" Mr. Simon was the president of a local charity that would have a float in the parade, and he already knew Jordan was very excited about the upcoming event.

"It's been pretty hard to focus lately," replied Jordan. "Besides that, I've got another mystery to solve, so this year's Trout Fest is going to be extra exciting!"

Mr. Simon knew about Jordan's love for crime solving and he was eager to hear about her latest case. But before Jordan could share any details, a knock at the door made Mr. Simon go see who was visiting his house. When he stood, Jordan saw something on his bookshelf that made her jump from her seat in the living room and run toward a giant stack of books.

3 THE CRIME SCENE

When Mr. Simon went to the door, Jordan's big brown eyes caught a glimpse of a large, leather-bound book turned sideways on the shelf. To her surprise, the book had the same title as the one that was missing.

She knew Mr. Simon would never steal someone else's book, but she was curious if he knew how valuable this book was. Her dad said there were only a couple of copies left, and she couldn't believe Mr. Simon had one of the two copies!

When he returned from the door with a small box in hand, he said, "Sorry, Jordan, the UPS man dropped off a package for me. Now, tell me about this case of yours."

"That's OK, Mr. Simon," said Jordan. "But first, do you know how valuable this book is?" she said, holding up the leather bound copy of *Evangeline* she had found on his shelf.

When Mr. Simon went to the door, Jordan's big brown eyes caught a glimpse of a large, leather-bound book turned sideways on the shelf. To her surprise, the book had the same title as the one that was missing.

"That old thing?" smirked Mr. Simon. "Unfortunately, not very much. A few years ago I was learning how to make things with leather, and I thought I would try my hand at book covers. So I bought that old book from a garage sale for a dollar, and then tried to make a cover for it. I made a few mistakes, and realized it was hard working with leather. But since it was my first book cover, I decided to keep it on the shelf." He showed Jordan some of the mistakes he made with the cover, and that the book inside was actually a reprint of the original and definitely not autographed.

Jordan placed the book back on the shelf, and then told him her story about the missing book, the timing of events with this year's Trout Festival, and her concern that she only had a few days to solve the case.

"Well, if anyone can solve it, I'm sure you can, Peanut," Mr. Simon assured her. "Now, let's get some dessert, because I've heard that freshly made apple pie with ice cream is the best way to activate your brain cells," he said with a twinkle in his eye.

"Sounds good to me!" said Jordan as she ran to the kitchen table.

After dinner and dessert, Jordan's family left the Simons' and arrived home around 8:30. Jordan put on her purple fuzzy kitten pajamas, brushed her teeth and made sure her back pack was ready for school the next day. After that, she had about 15 minutes to think about the case before bedtime.

When Mr. C. came in to say goodnight to his daughter, they talked about the case together and tried to guess at the motive for the theft. Jordan made a little list of ideas in her notebook that included words like: jealousy, revenge, and greed. Mr. C. reminded her that anyone could have been involved, including a family member who knew the value of the book.

At 9pm, Mr. C. made Jordan put her notebook away, they said her nighttime prayers, and then he tucked her in for the night. Jordan's mind raced with details about the mystery and with a general excitement about everything that was going to be part of Trout Fest the next day. She wasn't sure she would be able to fall asleep.

When Jordan's mom woke her at 7am, she sprang from her bed and rushed to the kitchen for breakfast. Jordan wasn't usually a morning person, but on the day that represented the start of Trout Fest she had no time for dawdling in bed.

Jordan and her siblings quickly readied themselves for their half day of school and then headed downstairs to put on their shoes, before getting in the family van for the short drive to school. Jordan wore her favorite pair of purple leggings, a "Girl Power" t-shirt, and her new blue running shoes. Her brown hair was pulled back in a small pony tail held tight with a Blue Blazer ribbon representing her love for Kalkaska.

Jordan's school was the first stop on the morning commute and as she said farewell to her family, she was quickly greeted by Emmie.

"I've got some great news, JJ. I called Abby last night and she talked to her parents. We can go straight to her house after school. Her mom said we could have lunch there, and take some time to investigate the crime scene."

"That *is* great news," replied Jordan.

"Also, while the police took some time to look around the house, they left the scene pretty much untouched," continued Emmie. "In fact, the family hasn't even done much clean-up except for a small repair made to the window where the thief broke in."

"Today is going to be the looooooongest half-day ever," said Jordan with excitement. "Trout Fest starts! We have a full-fledged mystery to solve! And Abby's mom makes the best grilled cheese sandwiches ever!"

The two girls giggled and headed in to their class.

4 A STRANGE TWIST

Jordan was thankful it was only a half-day at school. Before she knew it, the last bell rang and she and her friends were dismissed from class. Jordan had already texted her mom to ask if she could go with Emmie to Abby's house, so after the bell the three girls began the 10-minute walk through the quaint downtown of Kalkaska. All were giddy about the weekend.

"I can't wait to go check out the midway tonight," said Emmie. "Do you remember last year when the three of us rode the ferris wheel together?"

"How could I forget?" exclaimed Abby. "JJ screamed like it was a roller coaster!"

"Hey, you know I'm a little afraid of heights," Jordan tried to defend herself.

All three girls burst out laughing at the fun memory. Jordan, Abby and Emmie walked side-by-side, with Abby in the middle. Abby was much taller than JJ and Emmie, and she was always dressed in cute, matching, super nice outfits.

"By the way, JJ, I forgot to tell you, but now there's another mystery to solve at our house," informed Abby.

Jordan's curiosity was instantly engaged. "When I was getting ready this morning," Abby continued, "my mom walked into the room with an item in her hand, and you'll never guess what it was."

"The snow boots I left there last weekend?" asked Jordan with a snicker.

"No. It was the book that was taken two nights ago! We can display the book for the Trout Fest finale after all," shared Abby.

Jordan was actually speechless for a moment. Why would someone break into a house, steal a book, and then break in again two nights later to return it?

"Seriously?" was all Jordan could muster.

"I know, it's totally weird," Abby respond. "But it's the same book, with the same leather cover on it, and my parents are both a little shocked to say the least. The person must have come in from the same window as before because the newly repaired lock was broken again. Dad says he's going to call in a professional to fix the window this time."

The girls walked in silence for a moment before Emmie spoke up. "Well, this case just became more interesting! I can't wait to check it out."

As the girls walked the last five minutes to Abby's house, Jordan's mind raced. Why steal a book and then replace it? Why risk breaking into someone's house a second time, to return something worth so much money? Did the criminal feel guilty about his theft and just return it? Was there something more devious going on? Was it a trick? Would he come back a third time? None of this made sense to the fifth-grade detective, but that wasn't about to stop her from trying to solve this case.

When the girls arrived at Abby's large, white, two-story house, they tossed their shoes in the front closet, ran to the kitchen, and were greeted with grilled cheese sandwiches. They talked excitedly with Abby's mom about Trout Fest and each of them discussed her favorite part.

Jordan finished her sandwich first. "Thank you, Mrs. Blanco, for the delicious sandwich. That really hit the spot."

"You're welcome, Jordan," said Mrs. Blanco. "I'm sure Abby told you about the strange gift we received this morning, but I still haven't touched the crime scene," she said sweetly. "If you'd like to investigate the area, I can show you where it is, little Miss Detective."

Jordan was so eager to see the scene of the crime that she didn't even wait for her friends to finish their food. She hopped off the kitchen stool and followed Mrs. Blanco into the living room.

"There's the window the thief came through," Mrs. Blanco said while pointing to one of three small-sized windows across the room, "and there's the bookshelf." The shelf was on the other side of the room, at the base of the stairs leading up to the second floor.

Jordan liked how Mrs. Blanco decorated her house. The living room was fairly large, but very clean and tidy. A white brick fireplace occupied one end of the room, and on the mantel above stood recent pictures of the Blanco family. The floral couches and chairs were neatly arranged to face the fireplace and TV. Nothing appeared disturbed from the robbery.

"Interesting," said Jordan as she pulled out her pink notebook and wrote a few notes. Jordan always carried around a few crime solving tools in her backpack, just in case she needed them to help her solve a case on the go.

First, she produced a small blue tape measure and measured the window opening at 18 inches. On this particular wall there were five windows, with two very large windows on each end and three much smaller windows in the middle. Jordan thought it was a little strange that the thief used one of the small windows to break in, instead of one of the larger windows. This meant the thief couldn't be a very large person. In fact, he would need to be very small, maybe even a child.

Next she used her phone to take a couple pictures of the broken latch and looked around the window ledges to see if there were any fingerprint smudges. She couldn't find any.

When Emmie entered the room, Jordan handed her one end of the tape measure and had her stand next to the window while she walked over to the bookcase. It was exactly 20 feet from the window to the shelf.

Jordan walked back over the super plush, and very stylish, light-colored carpet, to the window and carefully lifted it to look outside. The window screen was on the ground, but not damaged, and she could easily see it in the flowerbed below.

Jordan asked to see the book that was stolen. It reminded her of the book Mr. Simon had showed her, with intricate leather stitching and a nice glossy front. The cover was stiff but clearly looked old enough to be from the early 1900s, and the book it covered was definitely *Evangeline*.

She handed the book back to Mrs. Blanco. "This is all so strange," said Jordan, talking more to herself than the other people in the room. "Let's go outside and check out the flowerbed."

The three girls left Mrs. Blanco in the living room, put their shoes back on at the front door, and then walked outside and around to the back of the house. Jordan saw the window she had opened and walked carefully to the edge of the grass.

Mr. Blanco loved gardening, and his yard was always full of color after the spring thaw occurred. Usually a week or two after Trout Festival, the area warmed up enough to allow for him to start tilling the ground and planting his seasonal favorites. Right now, since the snows had just melted, only a few weeds showed any signs of life. Jordan knew those weeds wouldn't be sticking around for long in Mr. Blanco's flowerbed, and brightly colored tulips, beautiful pansies and an assortment of other freshly planted flowers would adorn this flowerbed.

"OK, girls, let's do some detective work here. See if you can find any clues that might help us solve this case," urged Jordan.

Jordan took a couple pictures of the area outside the window, and then began searching for anything that might give her a hint as to who took the book. But after looking around for several minutes, the girls produced nothing that would help them solve the crime right now.

"This case just gets stranger and stranger," said Jordan as the girls walked back into the house. "What are your parents going to do with the book now that they have it back?" she asked Abby.

"Dad has a safe at his office. He plans to take it there Monday morning and lock it up after he displays it at the Trout Fest grand finale. He said he won't take his eyes off of it until we can figure out who broke into our house. We just found out it's worth a lot of money, but even more, Mom and Dad love that it has been in the family for all these years. They don't want to sell it, but they don't want to lose it again, either."

"Do you have any ideas at all, JJ?" asked Emmie.

"I have one big idea right now," responded Jordan. "Let's head out to the midway and see what new rides are here this year!"

The girls all agreed that heading to the midway was a great idea. As they walked back into the Blanco house, Abby paused, then picked up a little green ceramic frog sitting in the bushes on the left side of the sidewalk leading to the front door. It had been resting under a dormant rose bush. This little sidewalk led from the driveway, to the front door, was slightly "S" shaped and was about 20 feet long.

"Are you bringing a pet to the midway?" teased Emmie. She was the practical joker in this group of friends, and almost always had something funny to say.

"Ha, ha, Emmie," replied Abby. "This little guy is a ceramic key holder—it has a spare key to our house that we use in case one of us loses our house key or is locked out. It's almost always under that rose bush," she said pointing to a taller, dormant bush on the right side of the s-shaped walkway.

"Well, it is a cute pet if you want to bring him," said Emmie, as she took the frog from Abby and gave it a little kiss. "Bummer … no prince!" The girls burst out laughing at Emmie's antics. Then Emmie placed it

"Well, it is a cute pet if you want to bring him," said Emmie, as she took the frog from Abby and gave it a little kiss. "Bummer … no prince!" The girls burst out laughing at Emmie's antics.

back under the larger rose bush on the right side of the path.

After checking in with Mrs. Blanco, the girls cleaned up their lunch mess and headed out the door to enjoy their first afternoon of Trout Fest.

5 THE CLUE IN THE MESSY BEDROOM

The trio loved seeing all the rides at the midway, including the ferris wheel that lights up with bright orange, blue and green lights, the crazy Gravitron that spins so fast you stick to the walls while music blares from the speakers, and of course, the giant swings that lift riders over 30 feet into the cool night sky! They also took time to check out the prizes from the pay-to-play games. Bells and buzzers rang out from the arcade, and the smells of corndogs, popcorn, and cotton candy made them hungry even though they had just eaten.

When Trout Fest wasn't filling the space, the area where the midway was set up was part of the county fields. On one side were baseball diamonds for the little league teams, and on the other was a soccer field that got plenty of use beginning in April. In fact, some of the booths for the flea market were set up right on top of one of the baseball infields.

The whole area was boxed in by the Kaliseum, the horse stables and the county offices. Jordan's family had a membership at the Kaliseum, where her parents and older brother loved to work out, and where she and Erin loved to swim in the community pool. A fun swim at the pool, including dozens of rides down the massive waterslide, was a great way to enjoy a cold wintery night in Kalkaska.

"I want that giant, fuzzy panda bear," exclaimed Emmie as she walked past a game where darts were thrown to pop balloons. "It's bigger than I am!"

"I want one of those elephant ears," said Jordan, "they smell so good!"

The girls ran into many of their friends from school, made plans for the rides they would all enjoy together, and then began walking back to Abby's house. They agreed to meet up again at 7pm, with their families, to enjoy the midway at night. Jordan always loved how festive the lights and crowds of the midway seemed when it was dark.

Jordan's mom came right at 4pm to pick up Jordan and Emmie. The girls said goodbye to Abby and her mom, and then hopped in Mrs. C.'s van for the 5-minute drive to their apartment complex. The whole drive was filled with talk about their plans for Trout Festival.

After dropping off Emmie at her home, Jordan's mom asked Jordan about the case. "It's crazy, Mom, but last night the thief broke into their house again and—you'll never guess—they returned the stolen book!"

Mrs. C. was definitely surprised by this new revelation, and asked, "That's so strange; what do you make of it?" Jordan's parents loved to ask questions of their young detective.

"It doesn't make any sense, Mom. I investigated the crime scene, measured windows and distances, took pictures of the area and I even held the book and took pictures of it, too. The whole thing is so bizarre," replied Jordan.

"Do you think it's possible the criminal felt guilty and just returned the book?" asked her mom.

"That's definitely my main theory. But then I have several other questions, like why break in to the house to return it? Why not just bundle it on the doorstep or leave it anonymously at Mr. Blanco's office? It's risky breaking in to the house again to return it, so why take the risk?"

"Those are great questions, Jordan. God sure gave you an inquisitive mind for these things. You know what we say..."

"I know," said Jordan with a playful eye roll. "Just keep looking at the facts, keep thinking about the possibilities, and the answer will usually show itself," she said in her best impersonation of her mom.

Both Jordan and her mom chuckled as they arrived upstairs in their apartment. Jordan's brother and sister were home, working on their afternoon chores. Jordan never liked doing chores, but especially on

Fridays because it was the day she had to do extra cleaning in her room.

"Hey, Mom, since today is the start of Trout Festival and all..." started Jordan.

"No, Honey," interrupted Mrs. C., "you still have to clean your room and start a load of laundry."

Jordan's head dropped in mock pain, and she marched to her bedroom to begin cleaning. Jordan loved playing with her toys but hated putting them away, and so her floor was littered with Littlest Pet Shop figurines and, of course, clothes from the last few days. She wasn't very good at putting clean clothes away, or putting dirty clothes in the laundry basket, for that matter.

As she surveyed the mess in her room, she noticed a clear path from the door to the bunkbeds that she and her sister shared. She smirked, thinking about how carefully she made messes so that she always had a well-marked path to the bed. Her dad often told her, "If you'd take as much care putting your stuff away as you do making a path, your room would never be a mess."

After ten minutes of tidying she came back to the kitchen, where her mom was setting out sliced meat and toasting bread for a sandwich-bar dinner. Mr. C. was home now and everyone gathered in the kitchen to eat. The family always circled up and prayed before dinner, and tonight it was Jordan's turn to pray.

When she said, "Amen," the kids grabbed their bread and began making their sandwiches. Jordan's dad inspected her room, expecting to see a mess. "Well, nice work in there, Jordan Joy." (He almost always called her by her full name.) "I was expecting to see a small path, and now it's a large path. In fact, I would almost call your room 'clean,'" he said with a hint of sarcasm.

"Ha, ha, Dad," replied Jordan. "Besides, I like my small path. I might line it with flowers next time," she quipped.

Jordan's sister jumped in, "It's my room too, you know, and I don't want to have to walk through a flower garden to get to bed!"

Jordan froze at Erin's words.

"I was just teasing you, Jordan," said Erin. "I'm pretty sure I knew you weren't really going to put a flower garden in our room."

"That's it!" said Jordan, as she set down her plate, rushed to her room and came out with her notebook and phone.

6 TROUBLING THOUGHTS

Jordan scribbled feverishly in her notebook and studied pictures on her phone. Jordan's family had learned not to ask too many questions of the mini-sleuth while she was working on clues to a case; she couldn't say anything coherent until she was done writing in her notebook.

After several minutes Jordan looked up and said, "Thank you, Erin, for that idea. You see, when you talked about walking through the flowerbed in order to get through our room, it reminded me of the flowerbed outside of the Blanco house where the thief broke the window and climbed in."

"So what does that have to do with your case?" asked Mrs. C.

"Well, I just pictured Erin walking to her bed through the flowers and in my head I could see her footprints in the flowerbed. I was imagining walking behind her and trying to land in her footsteps, when it hit me," said Jordan.

"When what hit you?" asked Joe.

"Look!" she exclaimed as she held up her phone for everyone to examine.

Jordan's phone showed a picture of the flowerbed outside Abby's house. There didn't seem to be anything particular about the photo, but Jordan's mom was the first to notice the clue Jordan had seen in the picture.

"I see it!" said Mrs. C. "Or, more accurately, I don't see it," she said with smirk.

The rest of the family tried a few guesses until Jordan couldn't contain herself anymore. "That's right, Mom. It's what you *can't* see in the picture: no foot prints! If the thief had been in the flowerbed when he broke the window, and then climbed into the house from that place, he would have left footprints in the flowerbed."

"Good observation, Jordan Joy," said Mr. C.

"Way to go, sis," said Joe.

"Now," Jordan said with a little less enthusiasm, "I'm not sure what to do next. We know the thief didn't enter the house from the window, but how did they get in? Why was the window broken? And none of it explains why they returned the book two nights later."

"Well, you can only solve this mystery one clue at a time," Mr. C. reminded his daughter. "Who knows, maybe another clue will show up as you keep daydreaming about flower beds!"

Jordan knew her dad was teasing her. His hair was black, but his goatee was starting to get some grey in it. He usually had a good disposition, and he regularly teased Jordan that the grey hair didn't develop until she became a detective!

After dinner was cleaned up and Joe had placed the dirty dishes in the dishwasher, Jordan and her family loaded up in the van and headed out to the midway. It was a few minutes after seven when Jordan finally met up with her friends at the pre-arranged spot.

"Hey, JJ, I thought you'd never get here," greeted Abby.

"Yeah, Abby and I were thinking of doing the ferris wheel without you so we didn't have to put up with your screaming!" joked Emmie.

Abby pretended to scream like Jordan and everyone burst out laughing.

The Midway was buzzing with people from all over town. Jordan's teacher Ms. Hermom was walking around with the sixth grade girls basketball coach. Ms. Hermom was an attractive woman who always wore fashionable clothes and JJ thought her dark framed glasses complimented her beautiful black, curly hair perfectly. Jordan also saw principal Mas with his wife and three children standing in line for the bumper cars.

While the girls joined the line for the Tilt-a-Whirl, Jordan explained the first clue in the case. Abby and Emmie were always amazed at how Jordan could find clues that others missed. When she was talking about a case, her already big brown eyes became so big and expressive, it was impossible not to pay attention and become involved.

Abby had some news to share, too. When her dad called the window installers to repair the broken window, they were able to come in the afternoon before her family left for the midway. They told him that the break on the lock was a little weird. They explained that if the window had been lifted from the outside, the top part of the locking mechanism would have broken, not the bottom part. The bottom part was attached to the window itself, but the top part was attached to the frame and that's where the break should have occurred if the window had been lifted open when the lock was latched. Besides that, they said, it would require a very strong person or some kind of tool to break the latch by lifting.

Apparently the repair to the lower part of the window couldn't be made without taking it to the shop, so they just replaced the lower part of the window with a new piece and took the broken one with them.

"That's very interesting," mused Jordan. "This case is getting stranger by the day."

Before the girls could say another word, they were flying around the Tilt-a-Whirl, spinning, laughing, and enjoying every moment of the ride. As the bright golden lights spun around them, and the speakers blared a classic Beach Boys song, each of the girl screamed with delight. When it ended, Abby and Jordan laughed hysterically at Emmie's naturally curly brown hair that was sticking out in every direction. Her hair was usually hard to tame, but after a spin on this ride, JJ said it looked like she had been struck by lightning!

Over the next hour, the girls enjoyed five or six different rides, and then met with their parents to see if they could buy an elephant ear snack to enjoy. When they sat down on a bench in the middle of the midway to eat their tasty treat, the girls made plans for Saturday.

"I say we come to the Trout Fest Flea Market in the morning, and then we can have lunch and find good seats for the parade," said Emmie.

"That sounds like a good idea to me," replied Jordan. "I just need to make sure I wake up early enough to do my Saturday morning chores and put away my laundry."

"Good point. I have a few chores to do tomorrow, too. Hey, let's all bring our own lunches," added Abby, "and then we can eat them while we're waiting for the parade to start."

With their plans made for the next day, the girls found their families and said goodbye to each other. Jordan and her family had to stop by the Family Fare grocery store to purchase some milk and bread before returning to their apartment.

Jordan and her siblings got ready for bed and, as usual, she was the first one to slide under the covers. Jordan's main blanket was as warm as it was beautiful, and she had actually purchased it the previous year at Trout Fest. She told everyone she, "just couldn't resist the dolphins" that were pictured swimming in tropical waters. She was tired after a long and exciting day, and she couldn't wait for day two of Trout Fest and another chance to solve this crazy mystery.

After her bedtime prayers, she had nearly dozed off when she had one last thought about the case: since the window wasn't broken from the outside, it must have been broken from the inside! Was it possible, she wondered, that the book was stolen by someone who entered the house from one of the doors? Tomorrow, Jordan would need to see if she could inspect the broken window at the window shop to confirm her theory. If her theory was right, it was possible the book was stolen by one of the Blancos' friends. That was not a happy thought.

7 THE BROKEN WINDOW

Saturday morning Jordan woke on her own, an event that only occurred twice a year: during Trout Fest and on Christmas morning. Her alarm clock read 7:37 when she sat up in bed, and even more surprising, her sister Erin still hadn't woken yet.

Jordan climbed down out of the top bunk and wandered into the kitchen. Her parents were both at the table enjoying a quiet breakfast, and Jordan could smell the bacon her mom had prepared for Saturday morning.

"Good morning, Jordan Joy," said her father. "How did you sleep last night?"

"Really well. Although I did have some crazy dreams about the case."

"Wow," exclaimed her mom, "you even dream about solving cases!"

Jordan smiled and sat down at the table while her mom fried an egg to go with the bacon. Jordan's mom was very pretty. She had fine brown hair with a light red tint. She was athletic and strong, and Jordan thought you could tell by looking at her that she enjoyed working out and eating well. She was quite a bit shorter than Jordan's dad, but Jordan always thought they were a perfect match.

As she waited for breakfast, Jordan asked, "After I do my morning chores, I'm going to pack a lunch so that Emmie, Abby, and I can eat after we pick out a great place to sit on the parade route. Is that OK?"

"Sounds like a good plan," said her dad.

"Oh, I was thinking about the case when I was lying in bed last night, and I was wondering if we could swing by the warehouse of the company that replaced Mr. Blanco's window yesterday?" Jordan asked her father.

"I can call him and find out who did the work. Why do you want to do that, Detective Jordan?" her dad asked with a puzzled look on his face.

"This may sound strange, but I really think the window was broken from inside the house, and not from outside as everyone initially thought. If I could look at the actual frame again, I might be able to confirm if someone was in the house when they broke the window, trying to make it look like they came from the outside," explained Jordan.

"That would be an interesting turn of events," said Mrs. C., as she placed Jordan's fried egg and bacon in front of her. "Now eat up, do your chores, and I'm sure we can get you over to look at the window before you meet the girls this morning."

Jordan ate her breakfast while reading a Garfield comic book, and then headed to the bathroom to change, brush her teeth and put up her light brown hair in a pony tail that squirted out the back of a Seattle Mariner's baseball hat. She emerged from the bathroom wearing skinny jeans, a cute shirt that pictured kittens wearing sunglasses, and a blue Kalkaska Blazers hoodie; today looked like it would be sunny, but still very cool.

For some reason, the cute little freckles on her face seemed to stand out even more today. Jordan's mom liked to say, "A face without freckles is like a night sky without stars." JJ definitely got her freckles from her mom.

Forgetting that her sister was still asleep, since Erin almost always woke up before Jordan, she returned to her room, turned on the light and began her morning chores. Suddenly Erin sat up in bed, stunned, and threw one of her fluffy stuffed animals at Jordan. "Well, apparently it's time for me to get up!" teased Erin.

Jordan immediately reached up and turned off the light, embarrassed that she had forgotten about her sister. Erin put on her glasses, hopped out of bed and said, "You're always a bit goofy when you have a case, little sis!" As she moved to the door she added, "And it's a good thing I can smell bacon this morning, or I might be a little grumpier!" Both girls laughed.

Turning the light back on, Jordan put the rest of her dirty clothes in the laundry basket and moved to the tiny laundry room to pull out a load of clothes from the dryer. The washer and dryer sat side-by-side and basically filled up the whole room. She went back into her room, folded the clothes, put them away, and made her bed. The purple comforter with the dolphins always seemed to get bunched up at the end of the bed each night, and her matching purple pillow usually ended up on the floor. Jordan wished she could use her phone to film herself during the night to see how much she actually moved while she slept. She even lined up all 31 of her stuffed animals; Jordan loved her stuffed animals.

Emptying the dishwasher was the last of her chores and, once that was completed, she asked her parents about leaving for the warehouse.

"Well, it looks like Mr. Blanco used a company in the Kalkaska Industrial Park, so let me grab the keys and my wallet, and we will head over there as soon as I'm done with my morning reading," said Mr. C.

Jordan was excited to get to Trout Fest and see her friends, but she was even more thrilled to be getting a look at this window. Quickly she made a lunch that included a peanut butter and jelly sandwich, a small baggie of Cheeze-It crackers, and three brownies to share with her friends. She went back into her room and grabbed her notebook, her phone, and her water bottle, and came back into the kitchen as her father put on a baseball hat with the logo of his favorite team and headed down the stairs to warm up the car.

The small Kalkaska Industrial Park was about three minutes from Jordan's house, and as they pulled in to the U-shaped warehouse district, her dad quickly located the shop of the window company that serviced the Blanco house.

The Industrial Park wasn't very large, but a number of businesses operated there. Jordan could see an excavation company that kept all of their big machinery stored in one lot, and across the parking lot of the window company, a large semi-truck was being loaded with furniture from another business. She was surprised at how much work was happening on a Saturday morning, especially *this* Saturday morning.

Outside the big warehouse doors of the window company, a giant float sat on a trailer. Several employees worked to put the finishing touches to their Trout Fest entry into the parade. Jordan thought the float looked great, as it was made to look like a giant open window. The workers riding on the float would be able to stand on a small bench behind the window and wave "outside" to the people on the parade route. The "inside" was decorated with blue sparkly paint and somehow they made it look as though the sun were shining on the window.

Next to the giant open window were three over-sized house plants and, Jordan also noticed, two 5-gallon buckets filled to the top with candy. One of her favorite parts of the parade was the bags filled with candy that she would take home afterward.

The owner of the shop was a man Jordan had seen at the library; like her, he was member of the Kalkaska County Friends of the Library group. He recognized Jordan and greeted her and Mr. C. as they strolled into the warehouse full of windows and frames and all kinds of other glass that Jordan wondered about their use.

"Hey, Jordan," said Mr. Johnson, "How can I help you this morning?"

"I love your float," replied Jordan, "and I hope you have some of that candy left when you pass my spot on route!" she said with a big grin.

"Oh, we've got plenty and, don't tell, but we have an extra 5-gallon bucket of candy in the cab of the truck just in case we run out," Mr. Johnson said with a wink.

Mr. C. stuck out his hand to shake Mr. Johnson's and said, "I called you earlier this morning about inspecting a window you pulled out of the Blanco house yesterday. Jordan here is a detective and she's hot on the trail of the person who broke into their house."

Mr. Johnson looked at Jordan with a hint of wonder and admiration. "Well, you are just full of surprises, young lady!" He led them to an area of the shop where a bunch of broken windows and frames were resting, organized by size, against a plywood wall.

"I actually helped pull out that window yesterday," said Mr. Johnson, "so I know exactly which one it is.

I'm glad you came by this morning, because on Monday we're taking all these old windows to the recycle center to make sure they are disposed of properly."

He led Jordan and her dad to the window from the Blanco house. "Be careful, the broken glass around here is very sharp, but feel free to inspect all you need, detective," he added playfully.

Jordan was amazed at how many windows were located in this part of the shop. It seemed like there were more here than you could put in all the houses in Kalkaska! There were big windows and small windows, round windows and even some shaped like triangles. She was amazed at the variety of windows she could see.

Jordan and her dad were standing at the far end of the warehouse, where all of the broken and replaced windows were sent. Like Mr. Johnson had said, JJ knew she had to be careful because there was broken glass everywhere. "I guess if you work with windows, you have to learn to watch out for broken glass," she said to herself.

Mr. C. thanked Mr. Johnson as the owner headed back over to his float to help attach a final trim piece to the giant red window frame.

"Interesting," said Jordan as she looked over the frame. Pulling out her phone, she took three close-up

Jordan and her dad were standing at the far end of the warehouse, where all of the broken and replaced windows were sent. Like Mr. Johnson had said, JJ knew she had to be careful because there was broken glass everywhere.

pictures of the locking mechanism and could see, just as she was told earlier, that the part of the lock that was attached to the window had been broken, not that part of the lock that was attached to the frame.

Looking closely at the place the break had occurred, she could see where Mr. Blanco had tried to glue the mechanism back together the first time, because some of the glue residue was still on the window ledge.

Then, a series of scrapes caught her eye. They were directly above the window portion where, presumably, the lock had been and, directly under the mechanism that was attached to the frame. The scratches were not too deep, but definitely caused by something with a sharp point. She also noticed that the tool must have been pretty flat, because it had to fit completely under the lock in order to break it by prying it up.

Jordan showed her dad the scrape marks, explained her theory about the tool that was used, and then made a number of notations in her notebook. When she finished, she said to her father, "That makes it almost certain that the thief didn't break in to the house from the window, but was already in the house when he broke the latch to make it look like someone came in from the outside!"

Mr. C. loved watching his daughter work on a case, and watching her arrange each clue in a way that she could use to solve the mystery.

Jordan was satisfied that she had found what she was looking for, so she and her dad thanked Mr. Johnson for his time. Before they left, Jordan took a couple of pictures of the float to text to her friends. She couldn't wait to see all the other floats that would be part of the big parade later in the day. From her research on the case, she remembered that almost all of the floats in the first Trout Fest were pulled by horses. She wondered whether *any* of them would be pulled by horses this year.

8 THE TROUT FEST PARADE

Leaving the shop, Jordan's dad dropped her off at the Trout Fest Flea Market, waiting a few minutes until Emmie and Abby showed up. Each year at Trout Fest, local vendors were invited to sell their handmade crafts, locally produced items, or even garage sale items. The flea market was a staple of each Trout Fest and was as varied and unique as the people who make up Kalkaska.

The flea market was set up in a large area of grass at the far end of the county fields, closest to the Kaliseum. Dozens of canopies and tents were set up for the vendors, some just large enough to cover a couple of tables and a register, and some of them big enough to hold hundreds of people. All the tents were white or grey, and they were arranged to create three or four different rows of booths for all the different kinds of vendors.

Jordan's dad waved goodbye to Jordan and said he and Mrs. C. would try to find her on the parade route. Jordan could barely contain herself when she saw her friends, and quickly explained the new details of her case. The girls listened to Jordan's info with interest and then began walking around the various booths of the flea market. The girls loved checking out the different vendors and individuals who sold items each year on this special weekend.

Emmie loved trying on all the different hats she saw, and the girls took silly selfies with each one she wore. Jordan oohed and awed over every stuffed animal she found and each time Abby teased her, "JJ, do you really need another stuffed animal?" Jordan always nodded yes.

Abby had long blonde hair like her mom, always had her nails done to perfection, and absolutely hated getting her fingers dirty. Emmie and Jordan always said she was a "Princess in waiting." She was also very fond of purses and jewelry, and loved checking out the vendors who made their own fashion products. In one shop they saw a lady making beautiful belts for women. She had bedazzled a belt on one end with a dozen pretty pink, green and purple jewels, and now she was punching holes through the leather on the other end, to make slots for the belt to buckle properly.

The girls watched her for several minutes as she used a medium-length tool to punch a small hole in the belt, and then a larger tool to expand the hole so that it could be used by the buckle. The lady was a Kalkaska native who had been selling her products at the flea market for years.

Jordan could tell the lady enjoyed having the girls show interest in her work. She told them that she had been selling items in the Trout Fest Flea Market for almost 20 years, and she never grew tired of this event.

She also explained the belt-making process to the girls while they continued to enjoy her work. When she was finished, Abby couldn't help herself. The belt was beautiful, and definitely made for a young girl. She asked the lady about the cost, and smiling sweetly at the trio of friends, the lady replied, "Normally these sell for $15, but today I'm running a special for the first customers of the day. So how about $7.50?"

Abby had a job walking her neighbor's dog every day after school, and she was good at saving her money. Today she had put $10 in her purse just in case she found something she had to have. Abby squealed with delight as she handed the woman a $10 bill and received back the belt and $2.50 in change.

Jordan teased, "Abby, do you really need another belt?" The girls all laughed as Abby quickly looped the belt through her jeans and wore it proudly as they continued their wandering.

The rest of the morning zipped by as the girls visited every booth, and each enjoyed their favorite treat from the food vendors. Jordan bought an elephant ear, of course, Emmie enjoyed a cup of hot chocolate and Abby picked up some cotton candy. They shared their treats, and finally headed out to Cedar Street to find a spot to enjoy lunch while they waited for the parade.

The girls watched her for several minutes as she used a
medium-length tool to punch a small hole in the belt, and then
a larger tool to expand the hole so that it could be used by the
buckle. The lady was a Kalkaska native who had been selling
her products at the flea market for years.

Surprisingly, the girls located a great spot right next to the giant concrete Trout Fountain in front of the Kalkaska County Museum. Today was the day the fountain was activated, and water shot up from all sides, and poured out from the giant trout's mouth. They were thrilled to find seating in the middle of the parade route. The three girls sat on the curb and pulled out their lunches.

Abby began fidgeting with her belt a little and, after a moment, pulled it off to look at something.

"What's wrong?" asked Emmie.

"Oh, I just realized that one of the holes on the belt didn't make it all the way through the leather. After the parade, let's stop by that booth again and I'll see if she can finish clearing it out. It's the hole that fits me perfectly."

"She was a nice woman, and I'm sure she will be glad to help," said Jordan with some certainty.

The girls talked about school, waved to many of their friends, classmates, and teachers, then became more excited as a volunteer handed out large plastic bags for the kids to collect the candy that each float would throw into the crowd.

Suddenly they heard the high school marching band begin playing, and out came the first float!

Cedar Street was the main road through town. While Kalkaska's "downtown" was only a couple blocks long, the parade stretched out to nearly five blocks, starting well past the old buildings that gave the downtown such a quaint feel. During the Trout Fest Parade, people lined the sidewalks on both sides of the four-lane street to cheer and clap for each float that passed.

The town of Kalkaska had endured a lot of change over the years. While always being a great place to enjoy the outdoors, the industry of the town had changed from manufacturing and logging in the early years, to car production and oil drilling a few decades back. Now Kalkaska, or as Jordan's dad like to say, "K-Town", was filled with mom and pop stores, lots of local small businesses and a strong sense of community pride.

The downtown district where the parade commenced, consisted of a number of old buildings, with very little consistency between them. The old hotel that now served as a feed store, looked like it might topple over if the wind was strong enough. It stood alone on one side of the street while the rest of the old buildings were all on the other side. Another old hotel was currently being renovated and JJ had heard that the building had a bowling alley in its basement.

While all the downtown buildings stood side-by-side with their walls connected, no two of them looked alike. The red brick building, with a rounded roof, housed a carpet company. The two story appliance shop, which used to house Kalkaska's only movie theater, was tall and block-like, with beige siding. The corner store that always had the best Christmas displays in its front windows was made of white brick, and the second floor was all offices or apartments. Across from the corner store stood a very old-looking concrete building, that years ago was home to Kalkaska's first bank; today it was a t-shirt shop.

Jordan loved her little town, and she thought the uniqueness of each building added to the character of the city. On day's like today, there were few places she would rather be than sitting on the sidewalks of K-Town with her best friends, watching the Trout Fest parade get under way!

The high school marching band always started the parade, but soon all the floats came by, producing their own sound from speakers and sound systems cleverly hidden by creative decorations.

The girls were thrilled that the parade had started, and they waved at the people on each float, trying to persuade them to throw candy at the girls. Not one float disappointed Jordan and her friends, and as the last of the 107 floats came down Cedar Street, the girls' plastic bags overflowed with candy.

"I can't believe how much candy we collected this year!" exclaimed Abby. "I think we do better here than we do on Halloween," she said with excitement.

"Yeah, we live in a great town where we get bags full of free candy in October and in April," observed Jordan.

"This bag is so heavy," said Emmie, "I think I'm going to have my parents take it home while we go back to the flea market."

"Great idea," agreed Jordan, "but I don't know if I can trust Joe not to eat any while I'm not home!" Joe was athletic and fit, and it always puzzled Jordan that he stayed trim despite his love for sweets. He was almost as tall as his dad, and he played basketball and baseball for the high school. He loved working out with the Simons' oldest boy, Kaz, and like all good big brothers, he enjoyed torturing his younger sisters, too.

After the girls gave their bags of candy to their parents, they set off once more for the flea market and the midway. As they walked, Jordan said worriedly, "I'm still so perplexed by this case and the timing of events. I'm afraid if we don't solve it before tomorrow night, when Trout Fest is over, then we may never catch the thief."

The other girls nodded in agreement, though everyone was tired from the long day they had enjoyed so far.

The three friends walked back through the flea market area as the vendors slowly returned to their booths and tables following the parade. The girls walked directly to the woman who had sold Abby the belt and, when they showed her the hole that wasn't fully punctured, she apologetically went to work fixing the problem.

Again the girls watched as she pulled out two slender tools; the first with a sharp pointed end that re-punctured the original hole, and the second that was slightly larger and could expand the hole.

In a flash of activity that surprised Abby, Jordan grabbed her phone and exclaimed, "Wait, that's it!"

Even the woman working on the belt seemed surprised by Jordan's outburst, and Emmie, clutching her chest, said, "JJ, you almost gave me a heart attack!"

"Sorry," replied Jordan slightly embarrassed, "but I think I know what kind of tool the thief used to break the window. Ma'am, are those tools used primarily in working with leather? Are they strong?"

"Yes, dear," said the woman, "we old-timers sometimes call these 'leather punches,' and they are very strong. I've had this one for over 40 years, and before that it belonged to my mother."

"May I hold it?" asked Jordan.

"Certainly," replied the puzzled woman as she handed it over to the sleuth.

Jordan grasped the tool and studied the pointed end carefully. Then she looked at one of the pictures of the scraped up window frame on her phone to see if the leather tool could have been used in the crime.

"I'm not certain," Jordan said, "but I think it's possible a tool like this was used when breaking the window

In a flash of activity that surprised Abby, Jordan grabbed her phone and exclaimed, "Wait, that's it!"

in your house, Abby. The tip looks like it could have made the marks on the window, and it certainly fits the profile of needing to be small, slender and very strong."

"Wow, JJ, I don't know how you do it! I never would have seen that clue in a million years," exclaimed Abby.

The woman working the leather booth was confused, and suddenly Emmie realized how impolite they were being, waving around her tool and talking about something of which she had no knowledge.

"Sorry, Ma'am," confessed Emmie. "JJ, here, is working on solving a case and she just realized that a tool like this might have helped a thief break into a house, well, sort of break in..." She paused, not wanting to explain that the thief actually didn't break in with the tool, but only made it *look* like a break in. She continued, "And so now we have a big clue to help us solve this soon."

"Well, I'm glad I could help," said the woman with a look of astonishment. "You girls are pretty clever to be solving a crime, but make sure you stay safe when working; criminals are not the type of people you want to cross."

Jordan thanked the kind woman and handed back her tool which she used to finish fixing Abby's belt. Then Jordan had an idea. "Let's walk through the flea market one more time, and see if anyone else here would have use for a leather punch like this one."

There were many vendors this year, and at least a couple of them were selling leather goods.

The girls split up to cover more ground rapidly. They had barely separated when Abby frantically began texting her friends to come over, quickly, to the row of tents behind the food wagons where she had found a possible suspect.

Jordan and Emmie were almost breathless when they came upon Abby and in an instant they understood why she had texted them to come so quickly. They were standing in a tent full of leather wallets, leather purses and leather belts, but what caught their attention most was a shelf with dozens and dozens of books covered in lovely leather covers. The girls just stared at the large shelf of books.

9 A CLOSE CALL

Jordan broke their stupor by asking Abby and Emmie to find out who ran the tent. While the girls tried to figure out who owned the shop, Jordan took out her phone to take pictures of a few of the book covers.

She grabbed a light brown cover off the shelf and studied it carefully. It reminded her of the one Mr. Simon had showed her from his bookshelf, but his was definitely much older than the ones she was looking at here. This cover was stiff and needed to be treated before it would be soft and smooth like the one at Mr. Simon's house.

Jordan noticed that the covers were made in a variety of colors, from light brown to yellow to black, and some were even reddish in nature. Some looked much older than the one she was holding, but several looked like they might have been made just this weekend.

She was startled when a tall, burly man, dressed in heavily stained jeans and a dark green flannel shirt, grabbed the cover out of her hands and spoke gruffly,

"Please don't scuff up our new leather covers. Can I help you with something, miss?"

Jordan had a way of not acting scared even when she was startled, so she quickly regained her composure and replied, "Oh, no thank you. I was just wondering if these covers were made here in Kalkaska or if they were brought in from somewhere else?" She knew that no one could sell handmade items in the Trout Fest Flea Market if they weren't made near Kalkaska.

"Yeah, I make them myself," said the man who seemed unnecessarily annoyed at Jordan's question.

"Oh, that's good to know. Do you work on them here at the tent? Can I see your work station? I'm really fascinated by things like this." Jordan said this truthfully, because she did love knowing how things were made.

"It's closing time," the man replied abruptly. "You girls should be getting home now."

Jordan thanked him for his time, and turned around to see Abby and Emmie waiting behind her. They looked terrified, and were glad to leave the tent.

"Well, he certainly wasn't very friendly," explained Jordan. "There is something very suspicious about the way he was watching over me."

"That was scary," said Emmie worriedly. "I don't want to see him again."

"Yeah," agreed Abby, "he definitely gave me the creeps. But somehow, I think JJ is going to be investigating him a little bit more, aren't you, JJ?"

Jordan smirked, "You bet I am. Something is definitely up with that man and his leatherwork."

The girls were a little jumpy after their encounter with the strange man, especially since he closed up shop before 5pm. It wasn't even dark yet, and most of the booths were going to be open until 6 or 7.

To calm their nerves, the three friends went back through the midway, played some games and won a small fluffy panda at the game with darts and balloons. It wasn't the large one Emmie had hoped to win, but Jordan and Abby were delighted to give her a smaller version to take home.

After the games they each called their parents and, one by one, made plans to go home. They all attended the same church in town, so they knew they would see each other in the morning.

"JJ, don't do anything I wouldn't do tonight, OK?" Emmie said, not convinced Jordan would listen.

"You know me," said Jordan with a smile.

"Yes, I do, and that's the problem," teased Emmie.

Each girl headed home. Jordan's parents dropped her off at the house and had her take a shower so she would be ready to go to church in the morning. Jordan didn't always like taking showers, but she knew it never did any good to debate with her parents.

She came out of the bathroom in her pajamas and discovered her mom and dad had gone into Traverse City to have dinner with some friends. Traverse City was a larger town about 30 minutes from Kalkaska. So Jordan grabbed her notebook and made some more notes about the case. She wrote down some details about the leather worker and glanced over the pictures she had taken that afternoon on her cell phone.

Jordan's notes were carefully arranged by date so that she could quickly find data when she needed it. Her notes sometimes included quick little sketches, as well as quotes from suspects and even, occasionally, giant question marks that she used to indicate something wasn't quite right. For this particular case, Jordan's notebook had several question marks written on several different pages. This was definitely one of the most challenging cases she had tried to solve.

Erin came into the room while Jordan was making notes and asked her little sister, "Well, did you come up with anything new today?"

"I think so," replied Jordan, "but I really need to get a better look at the last tent we were visiting today."

"Why don't you come with me?" asked Erin. "I'm walking back up the midway to hang out with Alex." (Alex was Abby's older sister.) "Mom and Dad said we could hang out under the lights until they come back around 9:30 tonight."

Jordan couldn't resist the chance to go back out one more time, so she changed back into some skinny jeans and a purple Old Navy t-shirt, and finished drying her freshly washed hair before putting on her favorite Kalkaska Blazers sweatshirt and a green windbreaker to fight the evening chill.

Jordan's family lived right in the middle of Kalkaska, so they were just a short walk from the midway. Their apartment complex was known by everyone as "the colorful apartments" because of the brightly colored buildings that made up each set of units. Jordan and her family lived in one of the red buildings.

The two sisters carefully navigated the streets and arrived at the midway 20 minutes before Erin was supposed to meet Alex. "It looks like the flea market is closed, sis," Erin pointed out to Jordan, "we'll have to come back tomorrow."

"Actually," Jordan began in a voice that made Erin suspect her sister already knew about the hours of the flea market, "I was kind of hoping it would be closed. I need to sneak inside a tent and inspect a work station without being seen."

Erin smiled as she replied, "Sis, you have a way of dragging me into these little cases of yours, don't you?"

Jordan giggled as she led her big sister on the shortest path to the leather worker's booth. As she had hoped, everyone had closed up their tents and the area was clear for her to inspect the tools of the man who spoke so gruffly to her.

Using the flashlights on their phones, Jordan and Erin lifted the full-length flaps on the tent and crawled underneath. It took a moment for their eyes to adjust as it was practically pitch black inside the tent with the flaps all the way down to the grass.

Once Jordan knew where they were in the tent, she worked her way around to the front edge where she realized this large tent was broken down into three separate sections. There was a large tarp down the middle that divided the tent in two parts, lengthwise, and then one side was divided by another tarp, side to side, to make it three separate rooms. It was like a giant rectangular room on one side, with two smaller square rooms on the other side of the middle tarp.

Jordan and Erin entered the tent in the large rectangle side, where most of the sale items were displayed, especially the larger purses and the shelf of books that Jordan had seen earlier. In the front section of the tent, the first of the two smaller sections, Jordan found smaller sale items like wallets and belts, along with a table where the register would be positioned.

Not seeing the area of the tent where the tools would be kept, she moved stealthily behind the last dividing tarp and finally found the room where the man who ran the booth must do most of his work. She could see a work bench, a couple of stools, dozens of tools on the table and in buckets around the table, and strangely, two shovels and a small pile of dirt that had been recently disturbed.

Using the flashlights on their phones, Jordan and Erin lifted the full-length flaps on the tent and crawled underneath. It took a moment for their eyes to adjust as it was practically pitch black inside the tent with the flaps all the way down to the grass.

Jordan noticed that this particular room was totally closed off to the rest of the tent, so that whoever worked back here would remain unseen from anyone else in the tent, even when everything else was wide open.

This part of the tent was cramped, too, full of things Jordan assumed must be part of the leather working business. The work bench filled up a third of the space, and the buckets of tools made it hard to move around much.

Jordan explained to Erin the type of tool she was looking for, and after a few moments of searching, Erin held up a tool identical to the one Jordan had seen in the booth where Abby had purchased her belt earlier that day.

"That has to be it, Erin. Thanks for your help," Jordan whispered. "This tool could be the one that broke the window in the Blancos' house."

The words had barely escaped Jordan's mouth when the two girls heard a couple of men talking as they entered the large rectangular room on the other side of the middle divider.

"Don't worry, Larry, no one is going to find out about the book this weekend." It was a voice she had not heard before. "We'll make sure it is loaded back on the truck with the rest of the leather goods tomorrow night when Trout Fest is over, and then we'll move it across the country and sell it before anyone realizes we have the original."

"OK, Chuck, but no mistakes," said another man. Jordan recognized his voice instantly as the man who had noticed her in the tent earlier that day. "There was a pesky little girl nosing around the tent this afternoon. I don't know what she was after, but I didn't like the way she was studying the books. I think she knows something. Besides, she was with the tall, skinny girl, the one with braces, who lives in the house that we robbed."

"Oh, are you worried about a little girl, Larry?" said his friend sarcastically. "Relax, this plan is foolproof." Mockingly he added, "Imagine what all the boys will think when they hear that Larry Wisdom was afraid of a little girl!"

By now the men had entered the tent and turned on the lights, and even Jordan and Erin's section of the tent lit up. Quickly and soundlessly, the sisters laid down the tool, scrambled to the edge and lifted up the heavy tent flaps to make their escape. Erin had barely rolled under and closed the flap when the men entered the room they had just left. Silently the girls ran back to the midway.

"That was too close for comfort, little sis!" Erin said excitedly. "Let's get out of here."

"You got it! Now, even though this mystery hasn't been solved yet, we know the names of two of the criminals: Larry and Chuck."

10 TWO MORE CLUES

Jordan's heart was racing but she was thankful to have picked up a couple of key clues into the mystery of the book. Now she had a few more questions and, just as she had suspected from the beginning of this case, those questions would need to be answered before Trout Fest ended on Sunday!

A lingering question bothered her about something the men said. They had plans to take the book back into their possession, and on some truck, by the time Trout Fest ended Sunday. This meant they were going to steal it again, but Jordan wondered whether it was going to be from the Blancos' house or from the book display on Sunday.

If it was going to be the Blanco house, they would have to strike tonight. Of course, the men had said they were certain no one would notice that the book was taken, so it didn't really make sense that it would be stolen from their home again.

Taking it from the book display would be really gutsy, and yet that seemed like the best option from what Jordan had heard from the men in the tent. When her parents picked her up, she would notify the Kalkaska County Sheriff of what she heard. Maybe they would have a police officer guard the book while it was on display.

Jordan knew she was on the brink of solving this mystery, but something was still missing. Worse yet, she knew time was ticking away and she didn't have many hours left in which to figure it all out.

Jordan enjoyed hanging out with her oldest sister Erin, and with her friends, but was glad when her parents texted Erin to let her know they were waiting in the parking lot. The girls said goodnight to everyone and then hopped in the car with Mr. and Mrs. C.

"I see you had a tag-a-long for the night, Erin," said Mrs. C.

"You know Jordan, Mom, she loves Trout Fest—and she needed another chance to do some crime solving in one of the flea market booths," said Erin.

"Oh?" said Mr. C. with a hint of concern.

Jordan explained the interaction she, Abby, and Emmie had experienced with the man in the leather goods tent, and then described how she and Erin slipped in to take another peek. Mr. C. wasn't pleased that his daughters had done that without notifying them, but he was thankful they were safe.

"I need to call Sheriff Pete Oskey tomorrow and ask him to put a police guard on that book during the finale and to arrest Larry and Chuck tomorrow," said Jordan as she finished up her story.

"Well, hold on, sweetheart," her dad said softly. "Remember, you didn't actually see the men talking tonight, right? And you don't have any recording of their voices or of their plans, correct? We can certainly tell Sheriff Oskey that we think someone might try to steal that valuable book, but without proof, we can't go around accusing people of crimes we're not sure they committed."

"What do you mean?" asked Jordan. "I heard them say it with my own ears. Ask Erin, she heard it too." Jordan was feeling very defensive.

"Oh, honey, I believe you heard those words tonight, but the law requires a process and it requires evidence. Apparently the men don't have the book, so technically they haven't stolen it, and we can't prove that they stole it four nights ago, either."

This frustrated the eleven-year-old detective, who wanted to go kick down Larry's door (if she knew where he lived), and haul him off to the county jail. But Jordan knew her father was right, and now she was even more frustrated because she had less than 24 hours to solve this mystery.

Back at home, Jordan added a few comments to her notebook, then studied her notes from the case for a few moments. She found one note that caused her to open the *Big Trout Black Gold* book again, and though she was sure she was on to something, she wasn't sure she had enough time to solve the case.

As her dad came in to tuck her into bed, she climbed on to the top bunk and found herself in tears. "Dad, it's just not fair," she said. "Those bad guys might get away with stealing that book, and even if they don't, it seems like they'll get away with being rotten people!"

"I know, sweetheart, sometimes it seems like bad people get away with their crimes and innocent people suffer. But remember, the Bible says that our deeds will find us out, and that means that eventually our bad deeds will catch up to us if we don't stop doing them, and start doing the right things."

This comforted Jordan a little, and after they said her nighttime prayers, she quickly fell asleep, snuggled into her warm comforter, surrounded by her 31 fluffy friends.

Sunday morning brought heavy rain, dark grey clouds, and a strong, cold wind blowing out of the north, but Jordan's family enjoyed a nice warm breakfast around the table before heading off to church.

When they arrived in the church parking lot, Jordan noticed that Emmie and her family had just entered the building. That was unusual, because her family was usually a few minutes late. Emmie's curly hair was pulled back, and she wore a long, light blue dress similar to the long red dress JJ was wearing.

Mr. C. dropped everyone off at the entrance and then parked the car so that no one had to walk in the rain. Jordan quickly found Emmie and immediately filled her in on the case as the two girls walked to their Sunday School class. Once inside the room, they were caught up in a fun welcome game and some lively music, and soon both girls forgot about the troubles surrounding the Blanco family book.

When church was over, Jordan found her family in the church foyer and, after talking to "everybody we see" (as Jordan loved to lament), they loaded back in the car and drove off to lunch. One Sunday a month the family went out to eat after church, and today they found themselves enjoying pizza and salad at G's Pizzeria.

The afternoon weather improved a little. The sky was covered in light grey clouds and even a few patches of blue emerged. Jordan was hopeful that the sky would be totally clear before the start of the big firework finale that ended Trout Fest.

"What was your lesson about today?" Mrs. C. asked Jordan as the family sat down at a large table in the middle of the restaurant. Joe had attended the main service with his parents and Erin had helped out in the nursery with the little kids.

"Oh, we were talking about some people who lived in Israel a long time ago. Joshua was trying to take over the land for the Israelites and these people knew they were in big trouble. So instead of trying to fight Joshua and his army, they tricked them by carrying moldy bread, wearing super old clothes, and even by making their leather sandals look ancient. The trick worked, but only because..." Jordan stopped in mid-sentence.

"Only because giant pterodactyls came from the sky and ate all the bad guys!" said Joe as he finished his sister's sentence.

Jordan realized what her brother said and burst out laughing. "Not quite, big bro!"

"Sorry everyone, but I just had a thought. When we're done eating, can we make two quick stops? I think I just might have solved a big part of the Blanco book mystery!"

The family ate the rest of their meal, talking about church, the last day of Trout Fest and how thankful they were the rain had stopped. After Mr. C. paid for lunch, everyone headed back out to the car, eager to hear Jordan's thoughts about the mystery.

"First, can we swing by the Simons' house? I need to ask Mr. Simon a couple of questions about that book of his that's on the shelf."

Mr. C. dropped his family at the apartment, then drove Jordan over to the Simons' house, about five minutes from where they lived. Mr. and Mrs. Simon were out working with the horses they owned, and Jordan hopped out of the car and headed over to them.

The Simons had a nice house, nestled on a couple of acres on the outskirts of Kalkaska. They grew their own hay for the horses, and had plenty of room for their three dogs to get out and explore, as well as a mid-sized corral for the horses. Two small red barns housed the hay during the winter, as well as all the equipment needed to take care of the animals.

"Hello, Scotty," Jordan said, greeting a tall bay horse by name. Jordan loved animals, and especially horses. Her favorite horse, Bella, a light tan and white spotted Paso Fino, came by for a quick nuzzle and to see if Jordan had any peanuts. Bella loved peanuts and Jordan almost always had a handful ready for her. That was how she got her nickname from Mr. Simon.

"Hello to you, too, Peanut!" said Mr. Simon. "Now we see who your favorite family members are!"

Jordan laughed, and ran over to Mr. and Mrs. Simon and gave them both hugs. "Sorry," she said, "I'm always so excited to see the horses."

"So what brings you by the Simon house today?" asked Mrs. Simon. Mrs. Simon had straight blond hair, wore cute little glasses and was quite a bit shorter than her husband.

"Right, I almost forgot! I think I've had a break in the case that I've been working on, but I have a couple of questions about working with leather that I wanted to ask you," Jordan directed her words toward Mr. Simon.

"I'm not sure I can be of much help, but you can ask me anything you think might help the case," he replied.

"OK, so here's my first question: is it possible to make a leather book cover look older than it really is?" asked Jordan.

"That's a question I can answer," he said confidently. "The answer is yes, and that's exactly what I did to the book that's on my shelf in the living room. It's called 'distressing' the cover, and that's what a leather maker does to make a piece of leather look older than it really is."

"It's the same kind of thing people do to furniture, making old pieces look older or, as my dad used to say, 'giving it a little personality,'" added Mrs. Simon.

"That's exactly what I hoped you would say! Now, I have one more question and then my dad and I will need to make one more stop before heading back home," instructed Jordan. "Do people who work with leather leave a special mark that shows that it's theirs?"

"Most of them do; it's kind of like a way each one signs their work. You know how a painter signs his name in the corner of a painting? Well, most leather workers like to sign their work too, often in between the stitching of a project so that it's hard to see, though not if you know what you're looking for."

"Thanks, Mr. and Mrs. Simon, that's a huge help." With quick goodbye hugs for the Simons, and a fast nuzzle for Bella, Jordan grabbed her dad's hand and ran back to the car. As they climbed in, her father was curious where this clue was taking his young sleuth.

"If I'm right, Dad, then I think our next stop may almost wrap up this case. Let's go over to the Blanco house next and see if my hunch is right. If so, then we'll need Sheriff Oskey's help to set a trap for thieves."

A few minutes later Jordan and her dad pulled in to the driveway leading up to the Blanco's house. Jordan had texted Abby, who was outside waiting for them to arrive.

"JJ, what on earth did you figure out?" asked Abby.

"I can tell you in a few minutes," replied Jordan, "but first, I really need to take a look at your book. Is it still here?"

"Yes, my dad just pulled it off the shelf. Thanks to your phone call, Sheriff Oskey is coming to pick it up himself and make sure it's protected during the closing Trout Fest finale tonight," said Abby as the girls and Mr. C. walked into the house.

The two dads began talking about the case and the book as Jordan carefully opened the cover and inspected the stitching. She searched for several minutes using her magnifying glass before she made a discovery.

When she flipped to the back of the book and looked in the lower right corner of the stitching, she could faintly make out three letters. At first she thought they were just scratches, but after examining them thoroughly, Jordan realized she was looking at the letters C, L, and J, each one written between two parts of the stitching.

In the excitement of what happened next, she dropped the book and Mr. Blanco gently chided her, "Be careful, girls, that book is very old and very valuable."

"Sorry, Mr. Blanco, I guess I was a little excited," said Jordan apologetically as she picked up the book and placed it back on the table where it had been resting when she arrived in the house.

"OK, Dad, I'm ready to go. We have some work to do this afternoon before we go to the finale tonight, but I'm almost certain we will be able to catch the thieves before the fireworks go off," Jordan declared.

With that, Jordan and her dad left the Blanco house and headed home. As they entered their second-floor apartment dwelling, Jordan asked if everyone could join her in the front room. She was going to explain the case, and she was going to need some help to catch the thieves.

11 SETTING A TRAP

"OK, everyone, let me tell you what happened today and then I need to ask you, especially you Joe, to help me solve this case," said Jordan in her best girl detective voice.

"When we were at lunch and I was telling mom about the people who tricked Joshua by making their stuff look old, I had a sudden thought about the book at the Blancos' house: maybe the people who stole it tried to make it look old, too."

"Hate to break it to you, little sis, but it is old!" said Erin.

"You're right, the original book is old, but I wondered if the Blancos had a fake that was made to look old. So Dad and I stopped by the Simons after we dropped you guys off here, and Mr. Simon gave me two big clues. First, you can 'destress' a piece of leather"—

Her father interrupted, "It's called *distress*, Jordan Joy, not *destress*." Everyone laughed at Jordan's slip.

—"right, 'distress' a piece of leather to make it look older than it is. Then he told me that most good leather workers leave a signature of some kind, usually in the stitching, that tells you who made it."

"Oh," said Erin, "like how a painter signs his paintings!" Erin was artistic, and understood the importance of signing your works of art.

"Exactly right, big sis. So when we left the Simons', dad drove me over to the Blancos' while I texted Abby to see if I could inspect the book one more time. I studied it for several minutes before I found what I was looking for, the signature of the designer. Three letters were carefully carved in between the stitching on the back inside part of the cover. Only three: C, L, and J. The letters were written all fancy, so that they almost looked like scratches, but I'm sure it's the signature of the designer."

"That's when I dropped the book in my excitement," Jordan said with a little blush of embarrassment. "I didn't say anything then, but unfortunately, Mr. Blanco's book is a forgery and I'm pretty sure those guys we were listening to last night, Erin, are the guys who stole the book."

"Wait, what were their names again? Chuck and Larry?" asked Erin.

"Yeah, I wrote them down in my book so I wouldn't forget," answered Jordan. "So the initials in the book,

C and L, belong to those two. Now we need to figure out who the third member of their team is, and arrest all of them before they leave town with the real book!"

"So how do we do that?" asked Joe.

"I'm glad you asked," said Jordan with the kind of look that made Joe uncomfortable. "Because those guys saw me yesterday, and—who knows—may even have seen Erin last night, I need someone to create a diversion at their tent so that I can sneak in and inspect one of the other book covers on their shelf. If I can find the same C, L, and J on another cover, I can at least prove that they created the forgery."

"So you want me to create a diversion while you get your evidence?" asked Joe.

"You got it, big bro," Jordan replied with a smile. She knew how much Joe hated acting, but he was always willing to help out either of his sisters, especially if there might be some danger involved. Even though he didn't like to admit it, he was a little protective of both of his sisters.

"But Jordan," Mrs. C. chimed in, "proving they created the forgery and proving that they stole the book are two different problems. You still haven't solved the biggest issue. How did they get into the house if they didn't go through the window? They would have needed the key."

"I'm still working on that one, Mom, but for now if we can prove they created the forgery then maybe

Sheriff Oskey will have enough cause to search their vehicles and houses. That's what I'm hoping for," Jordan said thoughtfully.

Mr. C. and Joe went to work devising a scheme that would distract the men at the booth and give Jordan a moment to inspect one of the book covers. Erin and Jordan changed out of their Sunday clothes into something better suited for the Trout Fest finale, and for running should they get caught looking at the leather book covers. Mrs. C. put dinner in the crockpot so it would be ready when they came home. She hoped it would be a celebration of another case solved.

When everyone was ready, Jordan and her family headed downstairs to pile into their van for the short trip to the midway. The book display, part of the Grand Finale celebration, was happening upstairs at the Kaliseum, next to the art exhibit and several other Kalkaska County Fair and Trout Fest contest pieces, and would be open until 8pm. The fireworks would start at 8:30 and Trout Fest would be finished by 9 o'clock.

By the time her family reached the flea market on the other side of the midway, several of the vendors were already packing up their tents and booths and preparing to close up shop. Jordan's heart sank when she saw the booth with the leather works was almost completely emptied.

"Oh no!" she cried. "We might be too late!"

Mr. C. and Joe sprang into action and, as casually as possible, approached the front of the tent to inspect the scene. JJ's brother and dad looked alike, and she noticed they even walked the same as they approached the thieves. Sure enough, almost everything was loaded into boxes or crates, and all them were being loaded onto a giant cargo van. Mr. C. wondered if this was the van that would transport the Blancos' real book.

Joe saw a crate with several leather covers and casually picked one up. "Oh look," he said, "this would be a perfect gift for my sister!" Mr. C. was surprised at his son's approach, but quickly realized what he was doing.

"Are you sure? It seems like she might like a purse or something like that, son," he said in response.

"Are you kidding? She'd love this beautiful leather stitching and this is one of her favorite books," replied Joe. It was true that Jordan would enjoy the leather binding, but Joe wasn't quite sure if she had even heard of *Pride and Prejudice*; he didn't have much time to think while trying to trick the crooks.

One of the men taking down the stuff from inside the tent approached Joe and said, "Kid, this stuff's not for sale. We're packing up."

Joe didn't miss a beat. "Oh, come on, I'll pay you whatever it's worth. I have to get this for my sister," he said almost too sincerely, because he really did *have to get it* for his sister.

"Hey, Jake," the man said to his business partner in the tent, "how much for this cover? This kid wants it and I want this kid out of the way!" He was not a kind man.

Jake seemed irritated by the question but immediately understood the other man's tone. "25 bucks and not a penny less."

Joe pulled out his wallet knowing he only had $17 in there, but he was trying to stall to see what else might happen. His dad, realizing that Joe was going to be short, quickly pulled a $10 bill from his own wallet and handed it to Joe. "You'll have to help me wash the car next weekend to pay off that $10," he said sternly.

"Thanks, Pops!" said Joe, as he paid the man $25. The man carelessly stuffed the book into a plastic bag he snatched from a big box of miscellaneous items, and handed it to Joe.

When they had walked past several of the other tents, Joe let out a deep breath and looked at his dad with a huge sense of relief. "Good work, son, good work" said Mr. C. as he rubbed his son's head and roughed up his hair.

Joe found his sisters and mom waiting out of sight, back at the midway. With a big grin, Joe produced the leather cover from the bag the man had placed it in, and handed it to his sister. In a flash, Jordan had the cover opened to the back inside flap and with a look of triumph declared, "It has the same three initials!"

"And we now know," her father added, "that the J stands for Jake."

"Wow, you two make pretty good detectives. I might have to use you on one of my future cases," Jordan said with a smile.

"No thanks, little sis," said Joe. "That was absolutely terrifying!"

"Now that we've solved this part of the case, we have just a couple of hours to solve the next part and to locate the real Blanco book," Jordan said as she tried to pull everyone back together.

"Jordan," said Mr. C., "Mom and I will go up to the Kaliseum and tell the Blancos and Sheriff Oskey that the book is a fake. We will fill them in on the details, but I think they should keep the book on display, so that the three men don't become suspicious. For some reason they are waiting to leave until after Trout Fest, and if the book comes off display, they might get scared and leave before we can catch them."

"Good idea, Dad," replied Jordan.

"How about Erin and I try to catch a glimpse of the thieves' van and see if we can figure out where the real Blanco book is hiding? Maybe we can spot an obvious place where they would be keeping it so when it's time, we can reveal the true copy," said Joe.

"Sounds great," said Jordan. "In the meantime, I'll call Abby and see if we can figure out how the thieves got into their house without using a key..."

Jordan's voice trailed off as everyone left on their new assignments. "That's it!" she said to herself. Jordan pulled out her phone and frantically texted Abby: "When you come to the finale, bring the ceramic frog. But DO NOT open it!"

12 CAUGHT

By the time Abby met up with Jordan, frog in hand, Erin and Joe had made an important discovery. Mr. and Mrs. C. had informed Sheriff Oskey and the Blancos about the fake book, and they were all eager to see what the mini-sleuth had figured out.

"Jordan, the men packed up the tent and all the crates, but they kept out two shovels." Jordan scribbled a quick note in her notebook when Joe mentioned the two shovels. "Now they are just leaning against their van as if they're waiting for everyone else to finish cleaning up," reported Joe.

"There's no time to lose. Erin, you're the fastest in our family, so will you run and find Mom and Dad and Mr. and Mrs. Blanco?" asked Jordan. "Have them walk from the Kaliseum directly toward the van, making sure they block the road in case those guys have any idea of driving off in that direction. And please ask Sheriff Oskey to meet me over there," as she pointed to a security tent about 150 feet away from where the van was parked.

"You got it, little sis," said Erin. The family sprinter took off around the midway, toward the Kaliseum. She took the long way around to make sure she wouldn't be seen by the men standing next to their van. As she ran, her long blonde hair trailed behind her like a kite tail in the wind.

"Joe, you take Abby and her frog, and wait by the ferris wheel until I give you the signal that all is clear. When that happens, the two of you bring the frog over to the van. Make sure nothing happens to that frog, Abby," instructed Jordan. "And remember, do not open it or touch the key inside!"

"I'll take good care of it, JJ. Do you still think it might be Emmie's prince?" she asked with a smirk. Somehow, even when things were tense, Abby managed to crack a joke. The tall girl turned and began walking with Joe toward the ferris wheel.

Jordan knew she only had a couple of minutes to complete her trap and find the original Blanco book. She needed one more piece of evidence, and this would be the riskiest move of them all.

Jordan took a deep breath, said a silent prayer, and then walked straight to the van while holding the book her brother Joe had purchased for her. As she approached the three men standing suspiciously by the vehicle, she turned on the voice recorder of her phone and slipped it stealthily into her front pocket.

"Hi," she said a little too eagerly. "My brother just bought this book for me, and said it was from your tent. I think he mixed up the different tents. Is this really from your tent? Because I saw several leather workers at the flea market this year." She held out the book for the men to inspect by the last light of day.

"Hey, missy, that's our book. Now go find a good seat and watch the fireworks," the man named Chuck said to her in a tone that indicated he wasn't messing around.

"But how do you know it's yours?" asked Jordan. "It looks like all the other ones," she said, trying to be as naive and annoying as possible.

"Gimme the book," he ordered Jordan. Then he took it from her hand and opened it to the back. "Hey, Larry, give me a light." Larry produced a cigarette lighter from his back pocket and flicked it to life, giving Chuck enough light to show Jordan the three initials in between the stitching on the back page.

"There, you see that C, L, and J? That means that me, Larry, and Jake made it. It's a product of 'Wisdom Leather Works.' Now scram, kid, and go find a good seat for the fireworks."

As Larry could see Jordan more clearly from the glow of his lighter, he recognized her as the girl who had been in the tent the day before. His black eyes suddenly narrowed and Jordan felt the hair on the back of her neck begin to stand up.

"Hey, Chuck, this is the girl I was telling you about, and here she is again, snooping around our stuff," Larry told his partner in crime.

"Her, Larry?" Chuck asked, pointing a crooked finger at Jordan. "Hey, little girl, are you snooping around our stuff?" he asked Jordan almost mockingly. His bushy black beard added to the anger in his face. Jordan couldn't tell if he was about to snatch her up or laugh her off.

Jordan was terrified and realized she had made a terrible mistake in coming to the men by herself. She froze and didn't know what to say.

"Look at that, Larry, she can barely speak. I don't think she's much of a threat." Turning his angry gaze to Jordan and looming over her menacingly, "You better go home, little girl, it's getting dark and I don't want you to get hurt on the last day of this wonderful little event," he said with more than a hint of a threat.

Jordan turned around and began to walk away briskly. From behind Chuck spoke, "Hey, little girl, didn't you forget something?" Jordan turned to see he was holding her book in his hands. She hesitantly returned, grabbed the book and then spun around and almost ran away from the men at the van.

She was sure she was about cry and her legs were shaking in crazy fashion. She could hear the men laughing as she left them but she wasn't about to turn around again to see what they were doing. Carefully she pulled out her phone and turned off the voice recorder, then put it back in her pocket for safe keeping.

Jordan walked toward the back of the food booth selling elephant ears, swung around the front of it and then shot over to the security tent. Sheriff Pete Oskey was already there, and Jordan practically ran to him. He could tell she was shaken.

"Jordan, are you OK?" asked the kind police officer. Sheriff Oskey was a short man, but stocky. His light blue uniform seemed a little snug, and while he always greeted people with a smile, you had the sense that he wasn't a man to mess with if you were on the wrong side of the law.

"I'm OK, Sheriff, and now I have proof that those men made the fake book, and that they know where the real Blanco book is. At least, I think I do."

"This is serious business, Jordan, so let me hear all the facts as quickly as you can." Sheriff Oskey loved Jordan's crime-solving mind, but he was a good sheriff and knew the law well. He wasn't about to make an arrest without good evidence.

Jordan told him everything, and when the sheriff heard, from Jordan's voice recording, the men admit that the C, L, and J was their branding, he had enough evidence to arrest them, at least on the charge of breaking in to the Blanco house and leaving the fake book.

Sheriff Oskey called on the radio for backup and then walked toward the three men and their van, with Jordan staying safely behind him. As he approached, the men became a little concerned and when the sheriff called out, "Hey, gentlemen, I need to have a word with you," they scrambled to the front of the cargo van and tried to start it for a quick departure.

Sheriff Oskey ran toward the vehicle but as soon as the engine roared to life, the lights came on and revealed that Mr. and Mrs. C., along with Mr. and Mrs. Blanco were walking on the path directly in front of them. The three men had nowhere to go. Just then two deputies drove up behind the van and blocked it in from behind. The thieves were trapped.

It only took a few moments to get all three men out of the cab of the van. Sheriff Oskey arrested Chuck, while the other deputies put handcuffs on Larry and Jake. Chuck was arguing with Sheriff Oskey, "What did we do, sheriff? You can't arrest us without probable cause and we haven't done anything wrong!"

"You're under arrest for breaking in to the Blanco home and replacing their copy of the *Evangeline* book with a forgery," said Sheriff Oskey.

"We didn't break in to anyone's home!" argued Chuck.

With everyone gathered around, Jordan signaled for Joe and Abby to come over from the Ferris wheel. "Sheriff, they are right about that. They didn't technically break in to the Blanco home," Jordan said. At this, the sheriff looked alarmed.

Jordan continued, "But I believe that if you will carefully remove the key from inside this porcelain frog, you will find the fingerprints of one of these men on that key, and with the confession they made about the C, L, and J imprint on the book, you have enough evidence that they entered the Blanco house illegally and left the forged copy of the book."

The three men became suddenly silent and looked very concerned.

"And now, if my dad would take one of those shovels to dig under this small pile of dirt, I believe we will find where these men hid the book they stole from Mr. and Mrs. Blanco's house." Jordan stepped away from the pile of dirt she had seen in the tent when she and Erin entered the night before. The freshly moved dirt had bothered her, but it didn't make sense until Erin and Joe said the men were waiting by their vans with two shovels.

Mr. C. took up one shovel and a trooper named Charley Voy picked up the other, and in less than ten minutes of digging they struck something hard. A few minutes later they pulled up a small metal case. The case was locked, but a quick search of the men in custody produced a key that opened the lock. Opening the case, Sheriff Oskey found the actual book belonging to the Blancos carefully placed inside, wrapped in cloth and stored for safekeeping.

With this final piece of evidence, Sheriff Oskey and the two deputies secured the prisoners' handcuffs, read them their rights and moved them towards the police vehicles. Jordan saw Larry kick Chuck in the back of the leg while saying, "I told you that girl was trouble!"

*Mr. C. took up one shovel and a trooper named
Charley Voy picked up the other, and in less than
ten minutes of digging they struck something hard.
A few minutes later they pulled up a small metal case.*

As the officers hauled the prisoners off to the county jail, everyone else wanted to hear how Jordan solved the case.

"Well, it really came down to solving several small problems," began Jordan. "The first one was the problem of the broken window and the issue that it was so small. Most likely, someone who was breaking in through a window would have chosen one of the larger windows, and the fact there were no footprints in the flowerbed beneath the window made it improbable that someone came into the house through that path. Clearly, if the thieves had climbed in through the window, they would have left a trail."

"The second problem had to do with the leather of the book cover, and the fact that you can make leather look older than it is. When Mr. Simon helped me understand what destressing, I mean, distressing leather means, I inspected the fake book and realized it wasn't old at all. The cover had been distressed to make it look almost identical to the old cover, and the thieves did a good job. The mistake they made was that they used one of their old covers for the trick; they forgot that it was branded with their initials."

"But why did they break into our house to steal the book, and then break in again to replace it?" asked Mr. Blanco.

"I think they needed the original book to know how to make the fake book look more real. After they stole the real book, they used it so that the cover of the forgery would be hard to distinguish from the cover of the real book. The forgery was an attempt to make everyone think that the real book was back, and would be on display for the finale."

"With the fake book on display, there was no rush to leave town and raise any suspicion, so the three men could wait to take the real book and get out of town with everyone else. I believe they hoped the firework show would distract everyone so they could dig up the box and leave."

"OK, but how did you know about the key?" Abby wanted to know.

Jordan smiled big at that question. "That was the missing clue that I couldn't figure out until my mom mentioned something about them needing a key to get in, assuming they hadn't come through the window. That's when I remembered the frog had been moved from one side of the walkway to the other."

"While they scouted your house for the robbery, they must have seen someone use the frog to get into the house. I'm guessing when one of them grabbed the key to break in, he forgot which side of the walkway he had taken it from, so he accidentally placed it on the wrong side of the sidewalk as they left the house. Without that mistake, I'm not sure we ever would have figured out how they got into your home in the first place."

"I have to hand it to you, Jordan, you always find a way to take the clues, line them up, and then produce something that connects them all together. Way to go, lil' sis," beamed her sister Erin.

"I guess the only question I have left," asked her father thoughtfully, "is how on earth did these men know about the book?"

"This question stumped me until last night when Erin and I inspected the tent after hours," answered Jordan. "When the guys came in to the far side of the tent and began talking, I heard one of them call the other 'Larry Wisdom.'"

"That name rang a bell with me, so when I came home last night, before the lights were finally turned off, I reviewed my notes from the case and found the last name Wisdom from my studies of Kalkaska's history. They are a family that has been here for over 100 years."

"During the 1909 Kalkaska County Fair, the Wisdoms and the Blancos were winning many of the prizes from the various contests, and one newspaper writer suggested there might have been a rivalry between the two families."

"So when I heard that Larry's last name was Wisdom, I found in the book that his great grandfather's name was Lawrence, and I know that some guys named Lawrence also go by Larry. And guess what? Lawrence lost the writing contest to Abby's great, great grandmother, Abigail."

"Since the prizes from previous contests were announced as being on display for this year's event, I had a hunch that Larry decided to steal the prize that his great grandfather couldn't win."

"That was a pretty good hunch, little miss detective," said Mrs. C. as she hugged Jordan with just a hint of motherly pride.

Jordan enjoyed the thrill of solving a case, and everyone congratulated her on a job well done. Mr. Blanco was thrilled to have his book back, and everyone was glad the thieves had been caught and were on their way to jail.

As they prepared to leave the field and head home, the first of the fireworks shot into the air, lighting K-Town's night sky. The fireworks show was spectacular, one of the best Jordan remembered seeing. They stayed until the end, and it was a great finale.

When Jordan and her family finally arrived at home, she was exhausted, but very happy. The smell of ham in the crockpot filled the air and as she washed up for dinner, she was already wondering if another case might soon come her way...

With this final piece of evidence, Sheriff Oskey
and the two deputies secured the prisoners'
handcuffs, read them their rights and moved them
towards the police vehicles. Jordan saw
Larry kick Chuck in the back of the leg while saying,
"I told you that girl was trouble!"

ABOUT THE AUTHOR

Joe Castañeda: Joe has written three other books (all non-fiction) and is the founder of Overboard Ministries. He and his wife Traci have been married for over 21 years and have three pretty amazing kids. They moved to Kalkaska in the summer of 2015 and have fallen in the love with "K-Town" and its awesome people. Originally transplanted from the west coast (Oregon), the Castañedas have learned to embrace the beautiful scenery and the true 4-season experience of northern Michigan.

Celina (CJ) Castañeda: CJ loves to read. A few summers ago she was challenged to read 100 books during the summer, and she did it! This is the first book she's written, and her love for reading contributed much of the content, especially in regards to character descriptions and plot development. When not reading or writing, you'll often find CJ hanging out at church, playing outside with her siblings, working with her 4H animals or enjoying snuggles with pet guinea pig, Marlie.

ABOUT THE K-TOWN
MYSTERY SERIES

From Joe Castañeda: When my two daughters were younger, I loved our nighttime ritual of reading a story before bed. We read lots of books together, ranging from Dr. Seuss classics to C.S. Lewis' Chronicles of Narnia. We had so much fun reading those books together, and the girls always laughed at my feeble attempts at doing voices for different characters.

As most children do (Even though most parents tell them to stop!), my daughters began to age, and we started looking for books that would satisfy both of their reading appetites, despite the three year age difference. When we stumbled upon the Nancy Drew mystery books, we found a winner.

Now our nighttime stories were filled with mystery, heroic acts of bravery and a strong female character that was moral, courageous and incredibly kind to everyone she encountered. Each night usually ended with one of my girls pleading, "Can we *please* read another chapter?!"

My girls are both teenagers now, and I don't get the chance to read to them as I once did. So this book began as a tribute to our story times, and when my youngest read the first few chapters, she was eager to join the writing team.

The main character, Jordan Joy, gets her name from the middle names of my two daughters. Most of JJ's attributes come from my youngest, while Erin's character is drawn primarily from my oldest daughter, and Joseph's character primarily from my son.

The backdrop for the K-Town series is our Northern Michigan home of Kalkaska. After living here just a few years, our whole family has fallen in love with this great community, and so the names of many buildings, businesses and events have been kept in tact as tangible reference points for locals.

Ultimately, though, this is a work of fiction, and while some of the names of places remain in use, the names of people have been created or altered to avoid any reference to actual families or individuals from Kalkaska's rich history.

One final note: if you are local to Kalkaska, or know this area in any way, you may find a few "easter eggs" hidden within the pages of the story. For example, at the time this book was written, the principal at Cherry Street Intermediate School was Mr. Moore. In Spanish, the word, *"mas"* is defined by the English word, "more." So Principal "Mas" is a play on the name of Principal "Moore." There are several fun little references to Kalkaska's people and history, but you'll have to search to find the rest of them on your own!

And again, apart from descriptions of my own family and a few close friends, any intentional reference to an individual's name is only intended to enhance this fictional story, and not to describe them, their character or their personal history in any way.

Celina and I sincerely hope you enjoy this book, and others in the K-Town Mystery Series. We thank God for the chance to be able to write this and share it with you. Remember, If you're a parent, take time to read these books to your children, you will be glad you did! If you're a child, take time to read this book to your parents, they will be glad you did!

Look for Jordan Joy's next K-Town Mystery book coming out soon and learn more about her and her adventures at: www.ktownmysteries.com